I0726531

This book belongs to

____

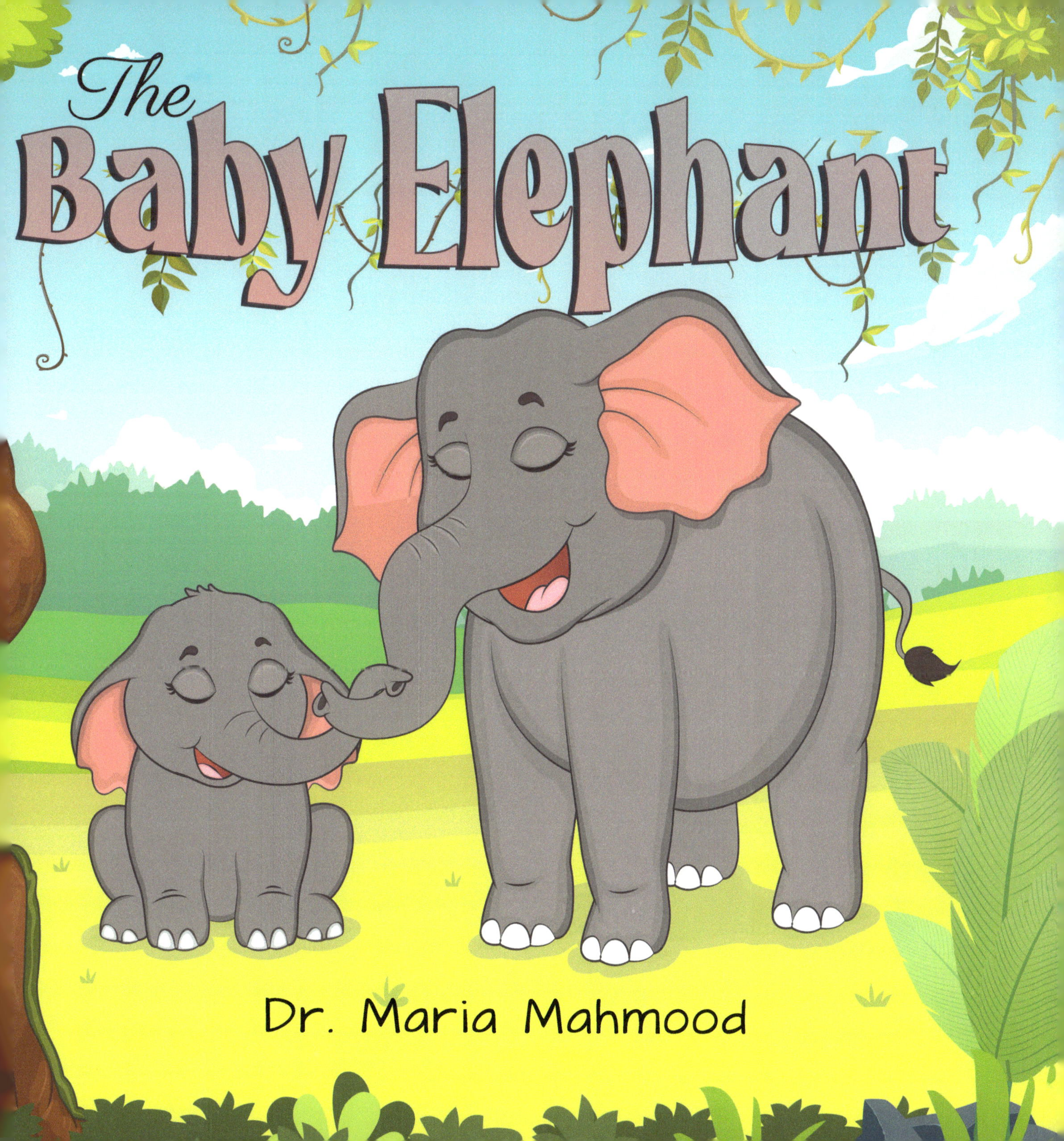

The
Baby Elephant
Dr. Maria Mahmood

Copyright © 2023 by Dr. Maria Mahmood

Paperback: 978-1-959224-46-4
eBook: 978-1-959224-47-1
Library of Congress Control Number: 2023900873

All rights reserved. No part of this publication may be reproduced,
distributed, or transmitted in any form or by any electronic or
mechanical means, without the prior written permission of the publisher,
except in the case of brief quotations embodied in critical reviews and
certain other noncommercial uses permitted by copyright law.

Ordering Information:

Prime Seven Media
518 Landmann St.
Tomah City, WI 54660

Printed in the United States of America

This book is dedicated to my boys, who will always
be my babies. May you always have a great love
for books and never run out of stories to read.

Love,
Mama.

Author's Note

This cute little story was created in the magical twilight
hours by a very sleepy Mommy with eyes halfclosed,
for a not-so sleepy Baby with eyes wide open.

Next morning Mommy had forgotten all about it until
Baby M started narrating the whole story to Daddy in
his sweet little voice and cute broken words. This made
me realise that even though Mommy was half-asleep when
she made up this story, Baby was not only awake and
listening but hanging on to every word. It just shows us
how very special these story-telling bonding moments are.

So I'm writing down this story for
it to last forever and ever.

Cheery Woods

Once upon a time, in Cheery woods, there lived a sweet little baby elephant with his Mama.

But this morning as he woke up rubbing his little eyes, he did not feel very cheerful. In fact, he felt..... sad !!
For he couldn't see his Mama anywhere..

The baby elephant was
very sad and very hungry,
But he decided to be brave,
So he set off to look for
his Mama..

He walked and walked through the woods, until he found Mr. Zebra.
"Mr. Zebra", he said in a timid little voice, "have you seen my Mama?"
Still munching on his grass Mr. Zebra replied, "No".

The poor baby elephant was still very sad and very hungry, but he braved on and kept walking..

Ahead in the bushes he heard a low roar and saw.....
MR. TIGER !!!!

Baby elephant put on a brave face and asked "M..m...m... Mr. Tiger please sir, have you seen my Mama?"

"Grrrrrrr", he replied, "No!"

And the baby elephant hurried away..

The poor baby elephant felt very sad and very hungry, but he braved on and kept walking,
He bumped into a pair of very long legs. He looked up and saw that it was Mr. Giraffe.
"Hello Mr. Giraffe", he said at the top of his lungs, "Have you seen my Mama?"

Mr. Giraffe looked down kindly at the sad little elephant.

"I have a very long neck", he said "I can look over the trees and find her for you".

He stretched his very long neck and looked around,

"Oh there she is, at the river, splashing in the water.."

"Oh thankyou Mr. Giraffe, Thankyou Thankyou", cried the baby elephant, finally cheering up!
So the baby elephant happily walked around the tall trees until he reached the river.

And there she was!
Mama elephant saw him and smiled,
"Come here my sweet little baby, look what I have for you"

"Mmmmmm", said the baby elephant, as he munched happily, hugging his Mama. "I love you baby" Mama said.
"Oh I love you Mama" said the baby as he snuggled.

About The Author:

Dr. Maria Mahmood is an Irish-born, Pakistani mum of two young boys. She took time off from her demanding medical career to be able to spend time with her beautiful family. Through her personal blog (nanhaybeej on Instagram) she encourages parents to give children the gift of their time and attention.

My sister and I grew up surrounded by books. I have beautiful memories of my father reading bedtime stories to us when we were little, and I want to create the same for the next generation.

Instagram:
https://instagram.com/nanhaybeej?igshid=YmMyMTA2M2Y=

www.ingramcontent.com/pod-product-compliance
Lightning Source LLC
Chambersburg PA
CBHW041924180726
48295CB00002B/70

ISBN 978-1-959224-46-4
9 781959 224464
90000

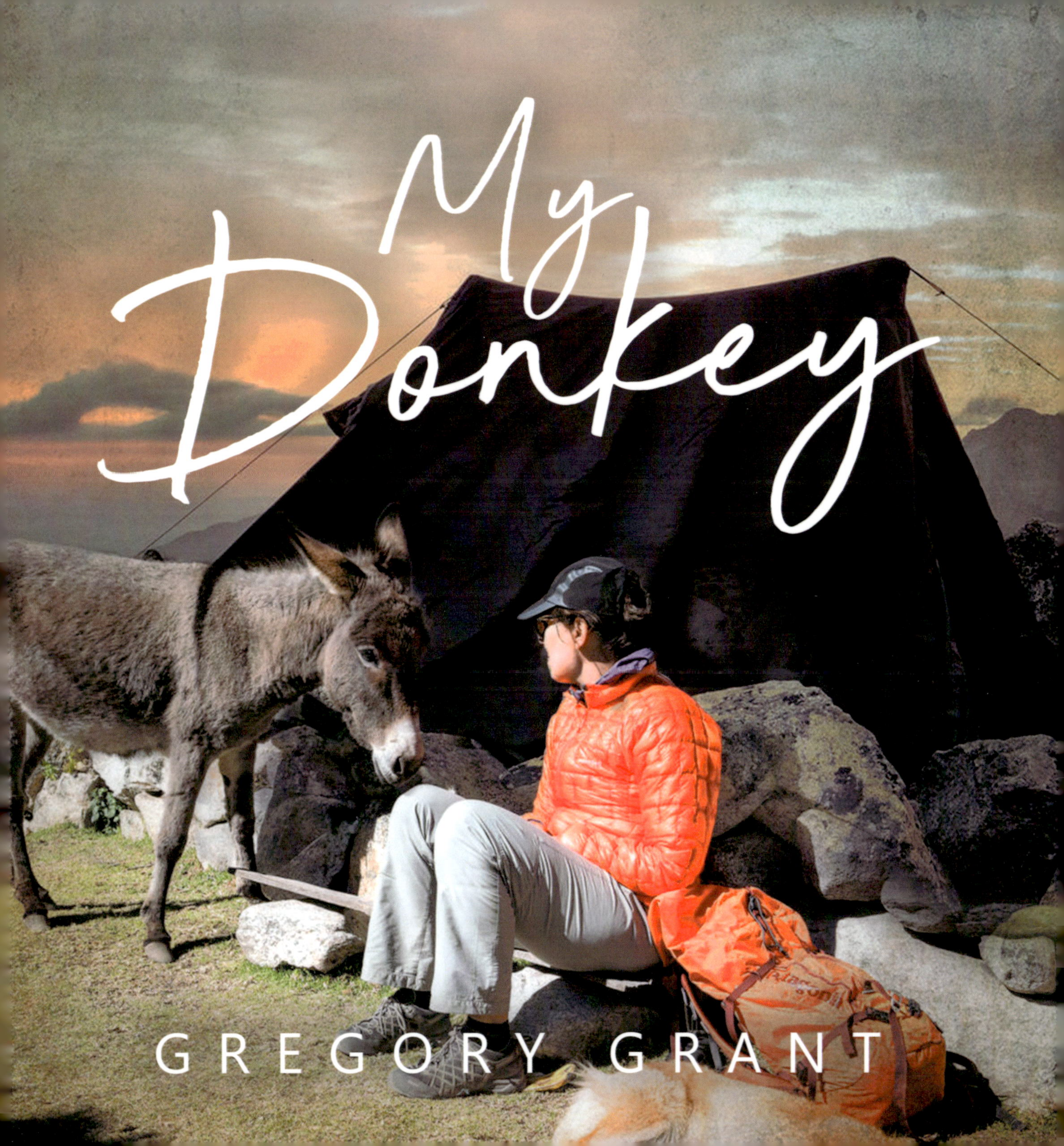

My
Donkey
GREGORY GRANT